CARLO COLLODI'S

PINOCCHIO

STONE ARCH BOOKS

MINNEAPOLIS   SAN DIEGO

CARLO COLLODI'S

PINOCCHIO

RETOLD BY **MARTIN POWELL**

ILLUSTRATED BY **ALFONSO RUIZ**

COLORED BY **JORGE GONZALEZ**

DESIGNER: **BOB LENTZ**

EDITOR: **DONALD LEMKE**

ASSOC. EDITOR: **SEAN TULIEN**

ART DIRECTOR: **BOB LENTZ**

CREATIVE DIRECTOR: **HEATHER KINDSETH**

EDITORIAL DIRECTOR: **MICHAEL DAHL**

Graphic Revolve is published by Stone Arch Books 151 Good Counsel Drive, P.O. Box 669 Mankato, Minnesota 56002 www.stonearchbooks.com Copyright © 2010 by Stone Arch Books All rights reserved. No part of this publication may be reproduced in whole or in part, or stored in a retrieval system, or transmitted in any form or by any means, electronic, mechanical, photocopying, recording, or otherwise, without written permission of the publisher.

Library of Congress Cataloging-in-Publication Data
Powell, Martin.
  Pinocchio / by Carlo Collodi ; retold by Martin Powell ; illustrated by Alfonso Ruiz.
    p. cm. -- (Graphic revolve)
  ISBN 978-1-4342-1583-3 (library binding) -- ISBN 978-1-4342-1738-7 (pbk.)
  1. Graphic novels. [1. Graphic novels. 2. Fairy tales. 3. Puppets--Fiction.] I. Ruiz, Alfonso, 1975- ill. II. Collodi, Carlo, 1826-1890. Avventure di Pinocchio. III. Title.
  PZ7.7.P69Pi 2010
  741.5'973--dc22   2009013684

Summary: Once upon a time, the dream of a lonely woodcutter is fulfilled when his puppet comes to life. Unfortunately, Pinocchio quickly becomes more of a prankster than a pleasure. He would rather create mischief and play tricks than keep up on his studies. Soon, however, the wooden puppet learns that being a real boy is much more complicated than simply having fun.

Printed in the United States of America in Stevens Point, Wisconsin.
102012   006968R

CONTENTS

CAST OF CHARACTERS

CRICKET

PINOCCHIO

Once upon a time there was a piece of wood.

It was just a common log, like the kind used in fireplaces or stoves.

But in the skillful hands of lonely old Geppetto, that piece of wood became a wonderful puppet.

Finally, I'm almost done! I'll call him . . . Pinocchio!

CHAPTER 1
THE WOODCUTTER'S PUPPET

Now exactly how the miracle came to happen, no one knows, but this puppet was no ordinary toy.

Why, I believe this is the best work I've ever done!

He nearly looks like a real boy!

Yes, indeed! I almost expect him to speak.

Hello, Poppa.

WINK!

9

Poppa! It started snowing while you were gone!

Yes, so it did.

What did you bring me?

I bought you a schoolbook, so you can go to school just like a real boy.

A book will do all that? It sounds like magic!

How does it work?

Oh! It's cold outside, Poppa. Where's your coat?

I sold it. It made me too warm.

My poor poppa sold his coat so he could buy me that book!

What will I do now?

It's going to be very cold this winter . . .

. . . and I feel sorry for your poppa. Take this money and buy him a new coat.

Oh, thank you, Mr. Puppeteer! Thank you so much!

Hurry home, now.

And try to be more thoughtful of your father . . . and a poor old puppeteer like me.

On Pinocchio's way home . . .

Good morning, Pinocchio . . .

How do you know my name?

Thank you for saving me from the robbers, Blue Fairy. You are very nice.

That was my wise old owl's doing. He brought you to me last night. He cut your ropes with his sharp talons.

You have another friend here to see you, as well.

Good morning, Pinocchio. You were lucky to have escaped those vicious thieves with your life.

I'm so sorry. I should have listened to you.

Poppa will be so disappointed in me.

Don't cry, Pinocchio. Your father will forgive you, because you are truly sorry for your mistakes.

He will?

Of course. He loves you very much.

27

Shouldn't we be going back to school now? I just heard the last bell ring.

Nah, that stuff's only for bookworms. I'm going to Playland instead. Wanna come along?

Playland? I've never heard of it.

It's a secret place where it's summer every day!

Boys do nothing but play from morning until night!

There are no books, no teachers, no bosses, and no bullies!

That's kind of hard to believe.

Well, seeing is believing, right? Take a look for yourself!

Soon, Pinocchio found himself in a wondrous land, where having fun was the only rule.

The puppet made many friends there, happily playing from dawn until dusk. In the months that passed, Pinocchio completely forgot about school . . .

. . . and about the promise he had made to his lost poppa.

CLACK!

CLAAACK!

CHAPTER 5
THE RINGMASTER

47

TYPES OF PUPPETS

MARIONETTES are kinds of puppets that are controlled from above using strings. These strings are usually connected to a metal or wooden rod that is held by the marionette puppeteer, or "manipulator." Marionettes are very difficult to use, because a combination of strings must be pulled to make the puppet perform simple movements.

VENTRILOQUIST DUMMIES are types of puppets that are controlled with one hand by way of a small glove attached to the puppet's back. They are called "dummies" because they can't speak — instead, the ventriloquist throws his voice and moves the dummy's mouth in sync, making it sound and look like the words are coming from the puppet's mouth.

CARNIVAL OR BODY PUPPETS are human-sized puppets that are used in parades and celebrations. One or more puppeteers move the body, arms, and legs. They are often used when the audience is far away, since they are easy to see from a distance. Big Bird from *Sesame Street* is a body puppet.

HAND PUPPETS are controlled by a single hand from inside the puppet. The puppeteer's hand controls the mouth and head, leaving the puppet's body to hang loosely over the puppeteer's arm. Other parts of the puppet, including eyelids, are often moveable as well. A sock puppet is a simplest type of hand puppet.

PUPPET TRIVIA

There is evidence that puppets were used in Egypt more than 4,000 years ago in 2,000 BC. Some historians believe puppets have even been used as far back as the year 30,000 BC!

In 1892, the great writer Oscar Wilde joked that puppets are ideal actors because "they never argue" and "they have no private lives."

Puppets were used in many royal courts to tell kings and queens bad news. Messengers, afraid of being hanged for saying something that would upset the king or queen, figured that they were less likely to be punished if the bad news was given by a puppet instead. Anything the puppet did or said could be dismissed as comedy, making it easier for a ruler to accept the bad news if it was upsetting.

In 1947, the TV show *Howdy Doody* introduced a marionette to Saturday-morning TV. The show was a big hit with children, airing until 1960.

The famous children's show *Sesame Street* began airing in 1969. It featured puppets called Muppets, which are a combination of puppets and marionettes. Big Bird and Oscar the Grouch are two of the shows most recognizable characters. *Sesame Street* episodes are still popular with kids to this day.

ABOUT THE AUTHOR

CARLO COLLODI was the pen name of Carlo Lorenzini. He was an Italian children's author who lived from November 24, 1826, to October 26, 1890. In 1880, Carlo began writing a story called "Le avventure di Pinocchio," which was published weekly in an Italian newspaper for children. In 1883, the entire collection of stories was published as a book called *The Adventures of Pinocchio*. Today, the book is considered a classic.

ABOUT THE RETELLING AUTHOR

MARTIN POWELL has been a freelance writer since 1986. He has written hundreds of stories, many of which have been published by Disney, Marvel, Tekno Comix, Moonstone Books, and others. In 1989, Powell received an Eisner Award nomination for his graphic novel *Scarlet in Gaslight*. This award is one of the highest comic book honors.

GLOSSARY

digested (dye-JEST-id)—broken down as food in the stomach

disobeying (diss-oh-BAY-ing)—going against the rules or someone's wishes

fairy (FAIR-ee)—a magical creature with wings who is often found in fairy tales

gigantic (jye-GAN-tik)—huge

grief (GREEF)—a feeling of great sadness

miracle (MEER-uh-kuhl)—an amazing event that cannot be explained by the laws of nature

recognized (REK-uhg-nized)—saw someone and knew who they were

ruined (ROO-ind)—lost wealth or was destroyed

stubborn (STUHB-urn)—not willing to give in or change

vicious (VISH-uhss)—cruel and mean, or evil and dangerous

wondrous (WUHN-druhss)—wonderful or remarkable

DISCUSSION QUESTIONS

1. Why do you think Pinocchio had such a hard time being good? Is he to blame for his mistakes, or is he innocent because he's new to the world? Discuss your answers.

2. Is it harder to be a kid or an adult? Why?

3. Each spread, or page, in a graphic novel has several panels, or illustrations. Which panel in this book is your favorite, and why?

WRITING PROMPTS

1. At the end of this book, Pinocchio has become a real, living boy. Write another chapter to this book about his adventures as a real boy. Where does he go? What does he do? You decide.

2. Miss Cat and Mr. Fox tricked Pinocchio. Have you ever been tricked? What happened? How were you tricked? How did it make you feel? Write about it.

3. The monstrous fisherman who catches Pinocchio plans on eating the little wooden puppet for breakfast. If you were Pinocchio, how could you have convinced him to let you go? Write about the conversation you'd have with the monster.

STONE ARCH BOOKS

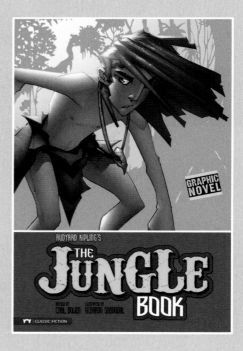

ALICE IN WONDERLAND

One day, a young girl named Alice spots a frantic White Rabbit wearing a waistcoat and carrying a pocket watch. She follows the hurried creature down a hole into the magical world of Wonderland. While there, Alice meets more crazy creatures, and plays a twisted game of croquet with the Queen of Hearts. But when the Queen turns against her, this dream-like world quickly becomes a nightmare.

THE JUNGLE BOOK

In the jungles of India, a pack of wolves discover a young boy. They name the boy Mowgli and protect him against dangers, including Shere Kan, the most savage tiger in the jungle. As Mowgli grows up, he learns the ways of the jungle from Bagheera the panther, the wise bear, Baloo, and other animals. Soon, he must decide whether to remain among beasts or embrace his own kind.

CLASSICS!

PINOCCHIO

Once upon a time, the dream of a lonely woodcutter is fulfilled when his puppet comes to life. Unfortunately, Pinocchio quickly becomes more of a prankster than a pleasure. He would rather create mischief and play tricks than keep up on his studies. Soon, however, the wooden puppet learns that being a real boy is much more complicated than simply having fun.

THE WIZARD OF OZ

On a bright summer day, a cyclone suddenly sweeps across the Kansas sky. A young girl named Dorothy and her dog, Toto, are carried up into the terrible storm. Far, far away, they crash down in a strange land called Oz. To return home, Dorothy must travel to the Emerald City and meet the all-powerful Wizard of Oz. But the journey won't be easy, and she'll need the help of a few good friends.

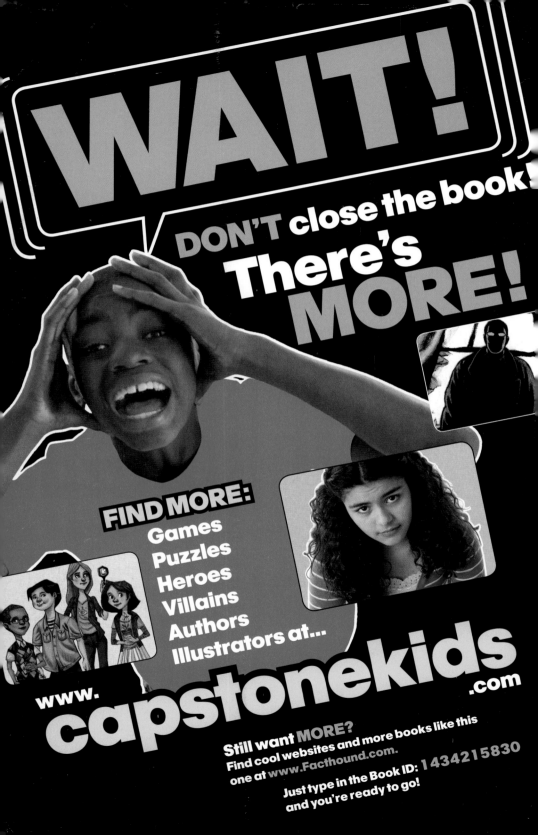